Dodo the unflighted swine
Flightless Birds
Tail 9

Tale & Imagery
Terry & Boyd Krueger

Puzzledmemorys Presses
KRUEGER PHOTOGRAPHY | DIGITAL DESIGN
©2021

WORKBOOK PRESS LLC
187 E Warm Springs Rd,
Suite B285, Las Vegas, NV 89119, USA

Website: https://workbookpress.com/
Hotline: 1-888-818-4856
Email: admin@workbookpress.com

Ordering Information:
Quantity sales. Special discounts are available on quantity purchases by corporations, associations, and others. For details, contact the publisher at the address above.

Library of Congress Control Number:
ISBN-13:   978-1-961845-93-0 (Paperback Version)
             978-1-961845-87-9 (Digital Version)

REV. DATE: 07.17.2023

Bill and Lon, thanks for the girls.

Sabrina, thank you for your penguins and diver.

After a full day of sampling and taking pictures with Dr. Nicky,
Dodo﹀ fell into bed. He was asleep before his head hit his pillow.

The next morning, he was up bright and early, ready to see what
the day would bring.

He went to find Dr. Nicky. She was already up and in the kitchen
preparing another warm breakfast.

Dodo˳ could get used to this...

As they ate their breakfast burrito, Dr. Nicky told him that today
would be very different and there would be lots
to learn and accomplish.

They would be spending the entire day in her lab.

Upon arrival, they carried all of the samples and supplies
into the lab.

First, Dr. Nicky said "Let's clean all of the equipment and supplies.
then put them away in their proper spots." She explained that
a successful lab, just as in one's own life, depends on everyone
being organized, following through on the details and being ready
to do it all over again, and again.

Once all was cleaned and put away. Dr. Nicky said, "I'll get you ready
to press your seaweed and I will process the samples we gathered
yesterday. We will also press samples for the herbarium."

Dodo~ began pressing seaweed.

He blissfully arranged, and then rearranged his seaweed.

"This is such fun. I still cannot believe this is called work."

Once Dodo was satisfied with the arrangement of his seaweed,
Dr. Nicky came over to finish it for him. She told him that the
next step was to lay a diaper liner over the seaweed. This helps to
prevent the seaweed from sticking to the top sheet in the press.
After that comes a stack of newsprint to absorb the moisture,
and finally a sheet of cardboard to provide some air in between
the pressings.

Once all of his pressings were orgainzed in the press,
Dr. Nicky tightened it all down.

"Now we wait until they are dried and then you can decide what
you want to do with them. Let me show you some pressings
which I have framed."

The framed pressings were beautiful. Dodo could hardly wait
for his pressings to be done.

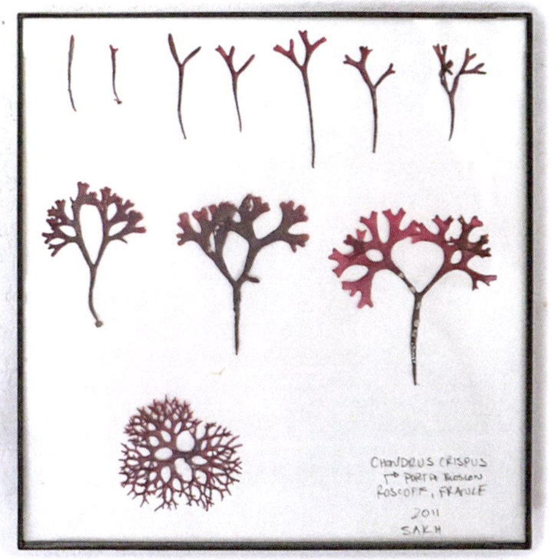

Dr. Nicky showed him the cabinet with her herbarium samples.

There they were, all pressed, labeled, organized and ready
for any future research.

Dr. Nicky told Dodo⸰ to come with her and to watch her
as she finished processing her samples.

Dodo⸰ followed her to the bench where she was processing
the seaweed. She sorted her seaweed, then took small pieces
of tissue and inspected them under a dissecting microscope, or
a hand-held magnifier. Next she placed some pieces of seaweed
into Falcon tubes for later DNA extractions and molecular analysis.

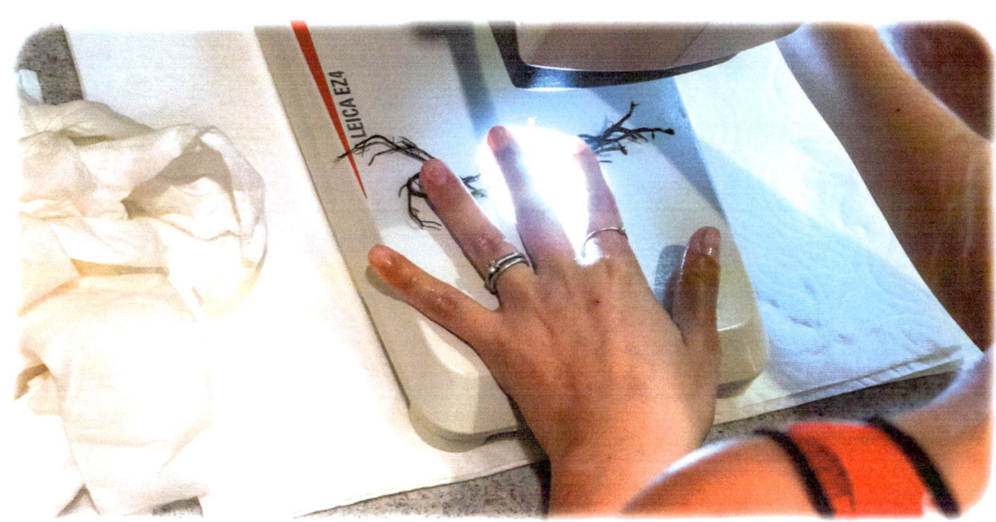

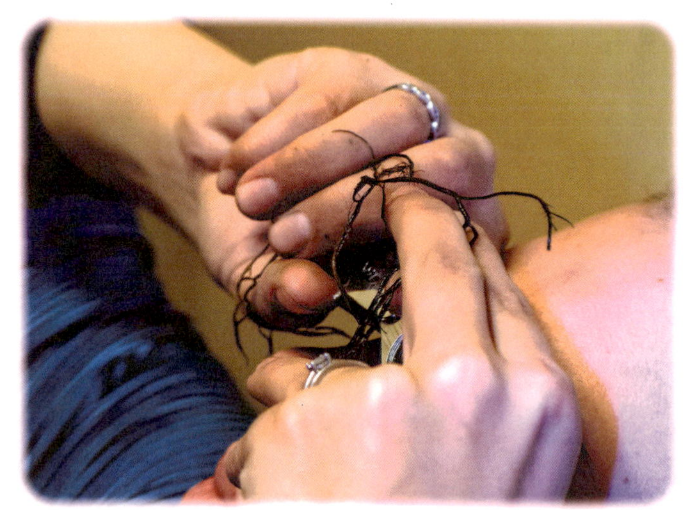

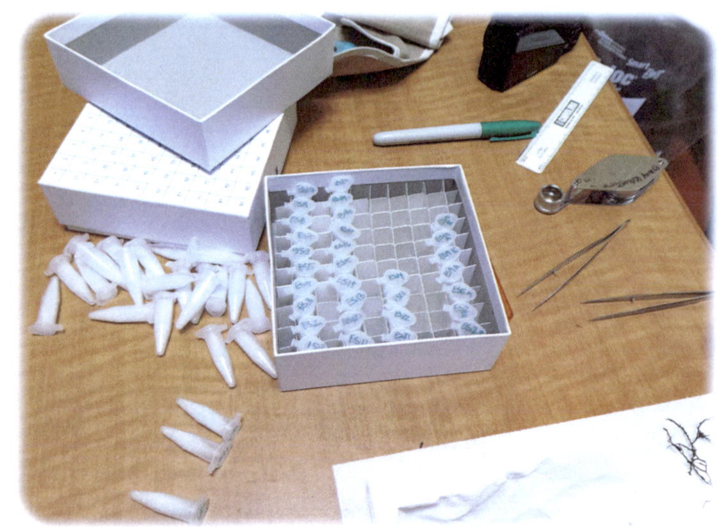

Yet another day during which Dodo was amazed at all
of the information he learned. And especially he was most
appreciative of the time Dr. Nicky spent to help him to
understand everything.

What good fortune had befallen him when Dr. Nicky rescued him
in the intertidal. Dodo asked if he might be able to see the
tattoos of which she had spoken ? He was absolutely certain
that he wanted to be returned to her if he got lost.

Dr. Nicky went to her computer and opened up the picture folder.
She said, "Here are some of my favorites."

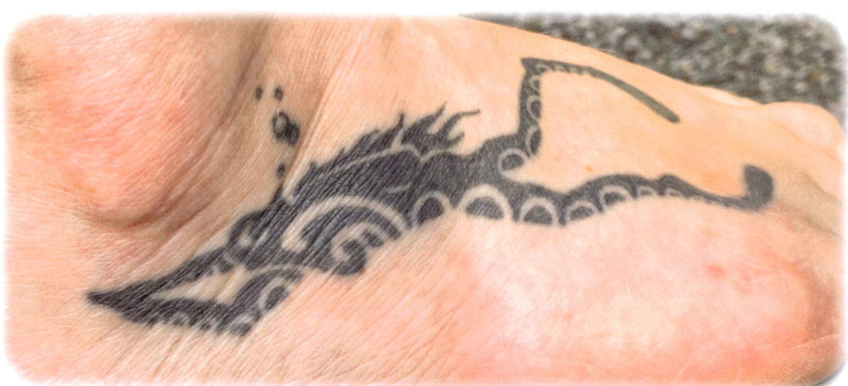

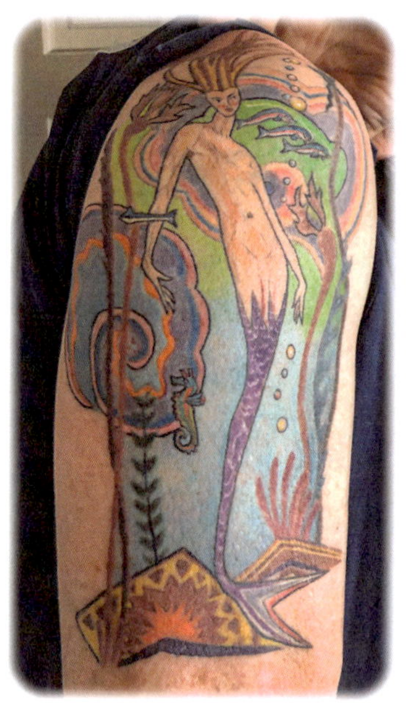

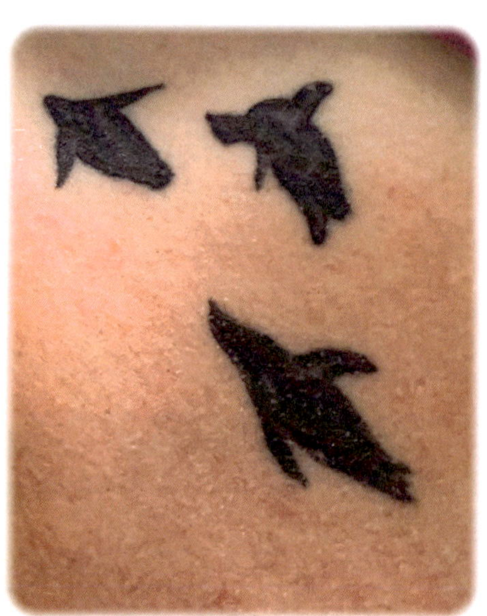

Dodo focused in on the birds.
"What are those birds ?"

Dr. Nicky explained that those are penguins; they can swim but they cannot fly.

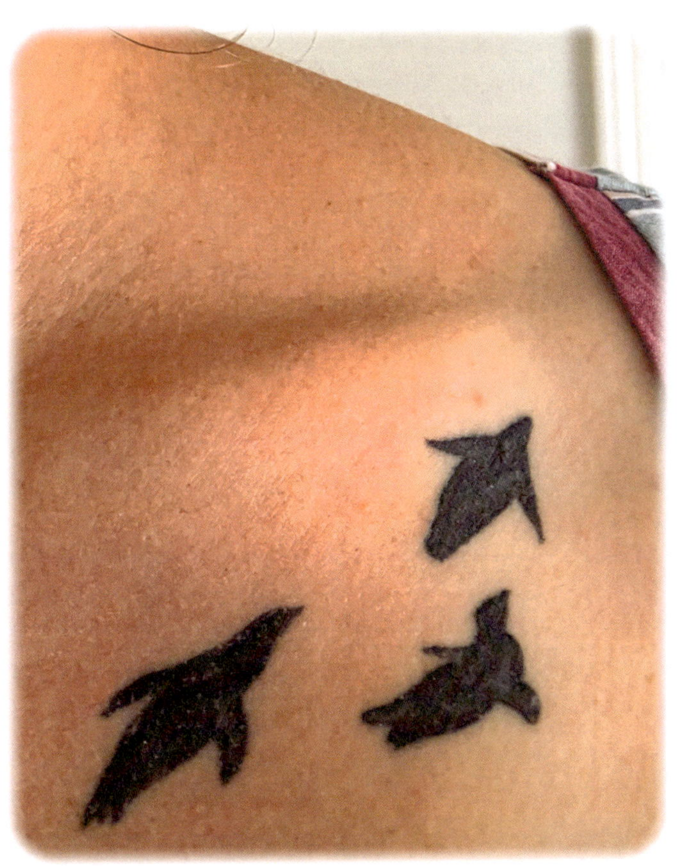

After a long stare, Dodo stated, "birds which cannot fly, but have wings and can swim. They sound a lot like me."

Dr. Nicky had not even thought about the similarity. "Penguins
are very interesting creatures. You really need to learn more
about them," she said.

"I am going to call one of my colleagues, Dr. Sabrina Adelie, PhD.
She has a vast knowlege concerning penguins and can tell you
all about them.
She has SCUBA dived all over the world so she can provide you with
a great deal of information, including facts which may surprise you."

They contacted Dr. Adelie and she said that she would enjoy
coming over to Dr. Nicky's to talk about penguins and her travels.
She was in her office and could come right over.

Dr. Adelie arrived with a satchel full of books and photographs
of flightless birds. After a proper introduction and some getting
to know one another, they went to Dr. Nicky's computer
and laid out Dr. Adelie's photographs.

Dodo~ could hardly believe all the new information he had
at his fingertips. One could have wings of all different sizes
and shapes and still be unable to fly. As he looked over the
information, he found his namesake.

He asked if he could see all of the information about the Dodo birds.
Then he settled in the learn about this extinct, flightless bird.

He was very pleased to have the name Dodo, and he really liked the
discovery of facts about his namesake. He thought that the Dodo
was a very handsome bird ! Having learned about the different birds
which had similarities to him, he did not feel so odd and alone.

Dodo asked Dr. Nicky, "Are you still willing to let me have your
phone number tattooed on me ?"

Dr. Nicky said she was more than willing. She wanted Dodo to always
know that her home is his home. He had a home with her now
and always would. He could come and go, but he would always have
his own room and a home with her.

That afternoon, they went to the tattoo parlor and once he had
his tattoo, he would never be lost again.
A very simple, "I'm lost" plus Dr. Nicky's phone number.

Dodo may just be an unflighted swine, with a strange appendage
protruding straight up from his back, a weird wing with
an odd twist at the tip... but, Dr. Nicky cares about him, and
he has a place to call home.

The next days were very, very busy in the lab and getting settled into his new life with Dr. Nicky. His tattoo healed up quickly and he proudly rolled over and showed it off to anyone who wanted to see it, as he had chosen to put it on his stomach.

Life was full of daily adventures. One morning Dr. Nicky said,
"Let's take a day off and just relax around the pool and enjoy
some sun." Dr. Nicky surprised Dodo with a handcarved
Dodo bird. Dodo floated on his raft for hours, just admiring
his gift. After much deliberation, he named his namesake
"Exmore." He thought his Dodo needed
a royal sounding name.

Then the news broke. A flu pandemic was affecting the whole world.

Life was changing yet again for Dodo°. This time, even though
"Stay at Home" and "Wear a Mask" orders were being enforced,
Dodo° was living with Dr. Nicky. All would work out
and they would be OK.

Dodo° had his mask and was ready to see what was coming.

Dr. Nicky said, "We can still work from my office here at home.
And Dodo°, you still have all of your photographs to go through.
We can get a lot of work done as we wait this out."

Dodo